The House That Jack Built

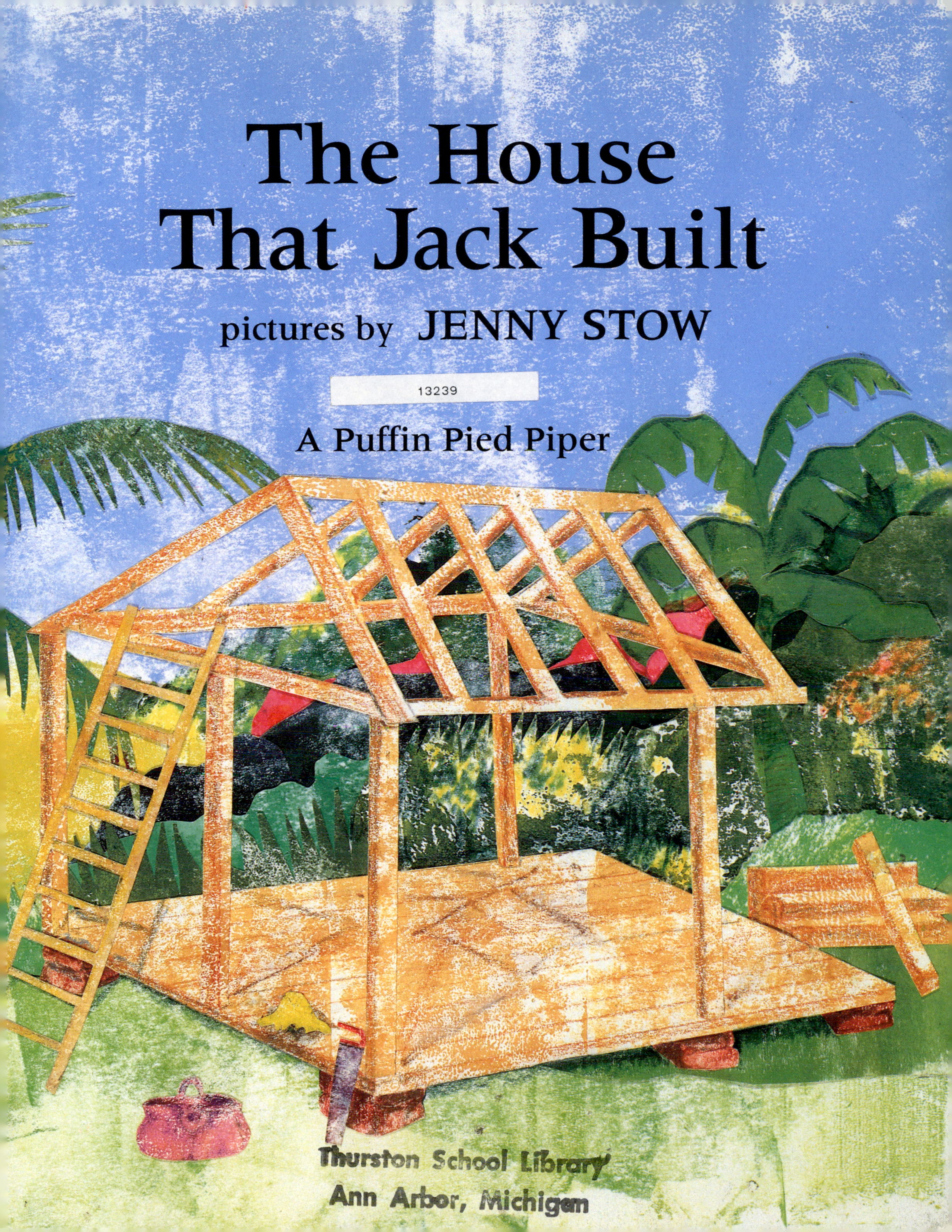
The House
That Jack Built
pictures by JENNY STOW
A Puffin Pied Piper

First published in the United States 1992
by Dial Books for Young Readers
A Division of Penguin Books USA Inc.
375 Hudson Street · New York, New York 10014

Published in Great Britain by Frances Lincoln Limited

Library of Congress Catalog Card Number: 91-23850
Printed in Hong Kong
First Pied Piper Printing 1993
ISBN 0-14-054590-5
10 9 8 7 6 5 4 3 2 1

A Pied Piper Book is a registered trademark of
Dial books for Young Readers,
a division of Penguin Books USA Inc.,
® TM 1,163,686 and ® TM 1,054,312.
THE HOUSE THAT JACK BUILT is also published in a
hardcover edition by Dial Books for Young Readers.

The illustrations for this book are collages rendered
in paint, ink, and crayon. To create different textures,
color was added using various techniques that
include rubbing, rolling, and sponging.

For Jack

This is the house that Jack built.

This is the malt
That lay in the house that Jack built.

This is the rat,
That ate the malt
That lay in the house that Jack built.

This is the cat,
That killed the rat,
That ate the malt
That lay in the house that Jack built.

This is the dog,
That worried the cat,
That killed the rat,
That ate the malt
That lay in the house that Jack built.

This is the cow with the crumpled horn,
That tossed the dog,
That worried the cat,
That killed the rat,
That ate the malt
That lay in the house that Jack built.

This is the maiden all forlorn,
That milked the cow with the crumpled horn,
That tossed the dog,
That worried the cat,
That killed the rat,
That ate the malt
That lay in the house that Jack built.

This is the man all tattered and torn,
That kissed the maiden all forlorn,
That milked the cow with the crumpled horn,
That tossed the dog,
That worried the cat,
That killed the rat,
That ate the malt
That lay in the house that Jack built.

This is the priest all shaven and shorn,
That married the man all tattered and torn,
That kissed the maiden all forlorn,
That milked the cow with the crumpled horn,
That tossed the dog,
That worried the cat,
That killed the rat,
That ate the malt
That lay in the house that Jack built.

This is the cock that crowed in the morn,
That waked the priest all shaven and shorn,
That married the man all tattered and torn,
That kissed the maiden all forlorn,
That milked the cow with the crumpled horn,
That tossed the dog,
That worried the cat,
That killed the rat,
That ate the malt
That lay in the house that Jack built.

This is the farmer sowing his corn,
That kept the cock that crowed in the morn,
That waked the priest all shaven and shorn,
That married the man all tattered and torn,
That kissed the maiden all forlorn,
That milked the cow with the crumpled horn,
That tossed the dog,
That worried the cat,
That killed the rat,
That ate the malt
That lay in the house that Jack built.

This is the house that Jack built.

About the Artist

Although Jenny Stow attended art school, before becoming a picture book illustrator she taught children with special needs. She then traveled extensively in Pakistan and in many countries throughout Europe and Africa, particularly The Gambia. She lived in Botswana in South Africa for three years and Antigua in the West Indies for one, during which time she traveled in the Caribbean and was inspired to draw and illustrate once more. Ms. Stow says, "New landscapes and people inspire my work. The flora and fauna, buildings, and colors that I saw in the Caribbean all contributed to the illustrations for this book." Ms. Stow is married with one son.